THE TOME OF TESTAMENTS
ADVERSARY

AN OUTERHELLS DARK URBAN FANTASY BY
JEREMIAH KLECKNER

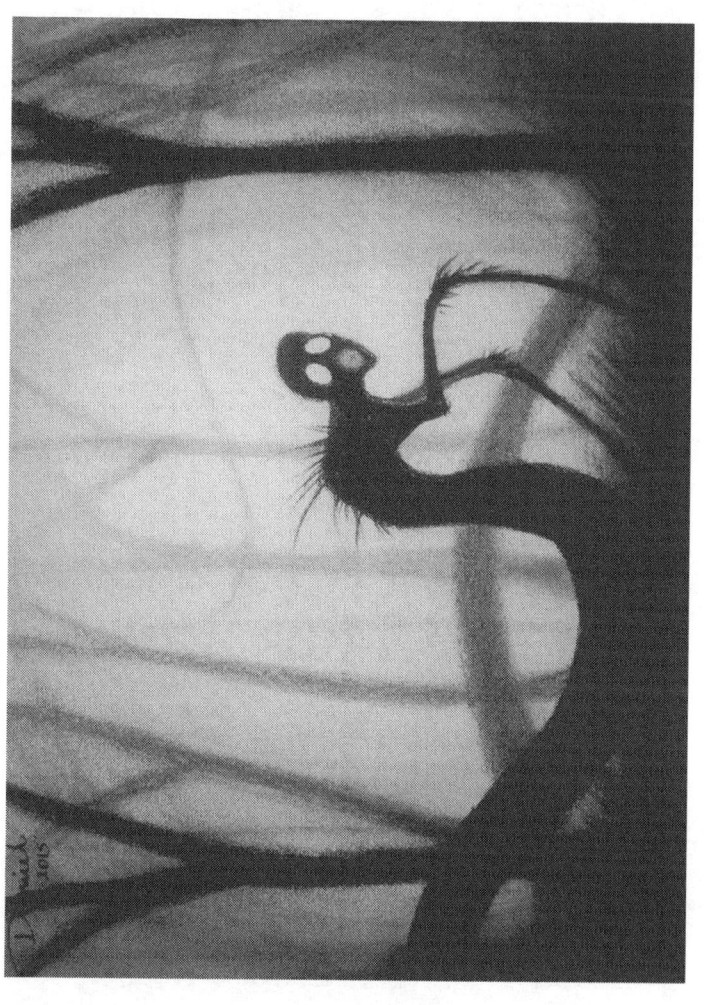

The Tome of Testaments ~ Adversary
An OUTER HELLS Dark Urban Fantasy
Copyright © 2015 Jeremiah Kleckner
Registration Number: TXu 1-967-091
Print Edition - All Rights Reserved
ISBN-13: 978-1522922193
ISBN-10: 1522922199

Crawler by Danny Brook (Artist)
Facebook: https://www.facebook.com/DannyBrookArt/

This is a fictional work and any resemblance to actual people living or dead, businesses, locales, or events is either coincidental or parodied with extreme absurdity.

Reproduction of this publication in part or whole without written consent is strictly prohibited.

Thank you for reading. Please consider leaving a review wherever you bought the book so that others may find it as well. Your support is everything.

The End.

Chapter One

Damon Nero sat for an hour before Rebecca walked into the narrow, dimly lit bar.

She suppressed a smile and looked over at the bartender. "Vodka and club with a splash of grapefruit."

The lean woman nodded.

Rebecca turned to Damon. "I haven't been here in forever."

"The last dive bar in downtown Hoboken," Damon said.

They hugged and kissed each other on the cheek.

The bartender set Rebecca's drink on a napkin. "Would you like to open a tab?"

"I'll take it on mine," Damon

said. The bartender nodded and wrote on a pad by the register.

Rebecca raised her glass. "To the end of year one of nursing school."

"To the end," Damon toasted.

They drank.

"Did you hear that Mark and Dion are out?" Rebecca asked, setting her glass down on the bar. A slow grin crept across her face.

"To be honest, I'm glad," Damon said. "From what little I knew of them, I wouldn't want either of them working on me."

Rebecca laughed. "It's scary how quickly people drop off between year one and year two."

The door opened and a chill rippled through Damon. It was subtle, only something he could sense. He straightened and looked around the bar.

A tall man with a ball cap and a flannel shirt walked in and sat in a corner booth. Damon reached into the man's thoughts, but found only a common staccato, measure for measure with the concerns of family and money.

"What's wrong?" Rebecca asked.

"There's a draft."

"In May?" she teased. "Do we have low blood pressure?"

"Are you going to check my vitals?"

She ran a finger through her dark hair. "I don't have my cuff with me."

"Maybe after the party," Damon said.

"Right," Rebecca said. She leaned back in her stool. "What time are we supposed to be there?"

"It started at eight."

Rebecca checked her phone. "Shit. How far is the house?"

"Right up Hudson."

They finished their drinks. Damon paid the check and they stepped out into the humid night air. They turned off of Washington onto

Second Street toward the water.

"How long have you known them?" Rebecca asked.

"Years now," Damon said. "Chris and Gracie have played a big role in my life."

"I'm still not sure how comfortable I am going to a party at one of my clinical instructors' houses."

They crossed Second. Damon savored the rare hum of solitude on the often busy street. "Your year is over. It'll be fine."

"She's just a little intense," she said, then caught herself. "No offense."

Damon laughed. "She has her moments. Just stay close."

"Oh." Rebecca smiled. "How close, exactly?"

They kissed and he felt the two-beat measure of her heart quicken and warm her slightly.

A hard thud blurred his vision.

He fell to a knee.

Rebecca screamed and her

delicate melody shattered into discord.

A second hit darkened Damon's sight into blackness and brought a loud ringing to his ears. Had Damon been mortal, a cracked skull would have been the end of him. But Damon Nero was not only far from mortal, he was far from description. The ringing settled to a dull tone and Damon shook away the last of his cloudiness.

Rebecca's muffled screams came from up ahead. There was a rustling, followed by silence. Damon followed the screams into the alley that Hoboken called Court Street.

The man in the baseball cap stood over Rebecca's prone body. He lifted one side of his flannel shirt and pulled an ornate dagger from his belt. The etchings caught Damon's eye.

The man was a Mithughee, one of many casts of hunters. How did he know where they would be? If he knew enough to go after Rebecca, how did he not mark Damon for what he was?

More questions sprang to Damon's mind, but he decided that the time for answers would come soon enough.

With unseen speed, Damon gripped the man's wrist and squeezed. Bones popped and cracked.

The man grunted through clenched teeth and the dagger fell to the cobblestone with a single clang.

Damon grabbed the hunter's throat and slammed his head against a dumpster. The man's eyes rolled into the back of his head. Damon thought the man had died right then and there, but the Mithughee stood on wobbly legs and clenched his fists.

Damon smiled. It had been years since he allowed himself to wear his truer skin. The change wasn't necessary. Damon knew that, but he allowed himself this one sadistic indulgence.

Damon felt himself grow taller, heavier. Colors, unseeable only seconds before, now alighted everything.

Two spirits stopped their midnight stroll through the ether, instantly aware that they too could be seen. One straightened its coat and cuffs, then hurried its partner along.

The Mithughee's eyes widened and he stepped back to run in terror. Damon outpaced the wind as he pounced.

Black claws struck forward.

Satisfied with his kill, Damon reverted to his common form and knelt beside Rebecca. A thin line of blood trickled down the side of her face, matting her hair. Thin breaths pushed past her lips.

Damon stalked back to the cooling body of his attacker. Oddly enough, the corpse continued to give off the same pattern of thought. *Money. Family. Career. Money. Family. Career.*

He pulled the man's shirt open and found a small pendant on a chain.

It had the symbol of the Mithughee on it, but held an opal in its center. The stone repeated its mundane thoughts at him. *Money. Family. Career.* It was an excellent camouflage for a hunter. Appear like one of the prey.

He lifted the man's body into a nearby dumpster and threw the dagger in as well.

Damon used his sleeve to wipe as much blood off of Rebecca's head as possible. Chris and Gracie's house was another couple of blocks uptown and he had to carry her without attracting attention.

Chapter Two

It didn't take Kevin Holmes long to get the call. The locals had eyes everywhere and it was only a matter of time before the next candidate was chosen.

Kevin walked the streets with his guides, a pleasant long-dead couple from 1920s Hoboken. They had a lot to say. He could only nod his understanding. Even long after the invention of wireless headsets, people were wary of those who appeared to be talking to themselves.

It still seemed odd to him to have to speak to the dead since they didn't speak out loud. They communicated, but they did so in a way that bypassed your ears.

He whispered when they stepped onto Court Street. "Where's the body?"

"Right here," the husband expressed. "Right in the trash."

"Horrible," the woman followed.

Kevin opened the lid and, under the thin layer of garbage, was a Mithughee. A young one, too. To be sure, he pulled the man's lower lip down and found the hunter's scar on the gum by the back molar.

"To be clear," the husband announced. "He attacked them."

Kevin turned to the spirit and raised an eyebrow. "There were two of them?"

"Yes," the wife added. "A man and a woman. Carrying on in the street, not caring who was watching."

Watching. The word struck Kevin with an idea. He held his hand up to quiet them and looked high on the walls. There, above the third window, was exactly what he needed. A slim black camera hung silently observing their every movement.

Kevin noted the address and walked around to the front of the building. He climbed the stone steps and rang the doorbell.

No shuffling footfalls. No barking.
He rang the doorbell again.
Nothing.

He scanned the front of the house for another camera and found one below the second-story window. Kevin walked around the back again.

Between his training and gifts, he took four minutes to access the house. Once inside, he found the security hub in the master bedroom. There were six camera hookups, four outside and two inside.

Kevin took out his phone and connected it to the hard drive. He cycled through the files. The backlogs carried a weight of information beyond the recording. Whoever owned the house hadn't reviewed the data in over a month. This was good. It meant that their habits were to only look when they suspected something was wrong.

Kevin reviewed the footage. It was a series of common images at first. People cutting through Court Street toward First or Second. A young couple embracing.

Then Kevin saw something amazing happen, something beyond description.

He uploaded the video to his phone and deleted everything from prior to that forward. He programed the system so that it would seem like the recording stopped before 8pm due to a loss of power.

Kevin left through the back door and dialed the number he had only ever had to call twice before.

There was a click and then a near-silent hush.

"You were right," Kevin said. "He's perfect.

Chapter Three

Gracie opened the door and gasped.

"I'm fine," Damon said. He pushed past the flood of her thoughts and rushed through the narrow hallway into the living room. "A Mithughee attacked us. He had a Hklfeha dagger."

Damon set Rebecca on the sofa and stepped back. Gracie pulled her hair into a ponytail, knelt beside Rebecca, and got to work checking her wounds.

A short, stalky man walked in from the kitchen, "What the hell happened?"

Damon turned to him. "They

know."

"How?" the man asked, bristling beneath his shirt.

"I don't know how they know, Chris, but they know," Damon said. "I couldn't read him when he snuck up on us. He had something with him. A pendant that sent out false thoughts even after he was dead."

Gracie looked up, concerned. "You didn't bring it here, did you?"

Damon scowled at her, then softened. "The body, knife, and pendant are all in a dumpster. They dispose of their own, so it'll all be gone in the morning." He motioned to Rebecca. "How is she?"

"Most of it is superficial," Gracie said, checking Rebecca's eyes. She then stood and walked into the kitchen. Damon heard the faucet run for a moment before she walked back into the living room with a wet towel. She cleaned the dirt and blood off of Rebecca's face and hands. "It doesn't look like she has a concussion. We were lucky."

"What do you think they wanted?" Chris asked.

"Considering the knife," Damon said, "my guess is that they wanted her dead."

"So we were right about her," Chris said, a smile grew on his face.

Damon smiled back. "I guess so."

"A call went out while you were gone," Gracie said. The words hung in the air for a minute. "You're requested at *The Tome*."

Damon nodded and walked upstairs to the second bedroom.

The Tome of Testaments looked just like any other book, except when it didn't. When Gracie used *The Tome* last week, it resembled a 1000 page dictionary. Chris stepped to *The Tome* one time and it lit up in holographic beauty. This time the book was flat, large, and old.

The cover flaked and cracked as

Damon pried the book open. It never mattered which page he turned to in *The Tome*, it was always blank. There was no looking back at pages he had seen before and there was no looking forward at pages he had yet to read. The Gods of the Far only ever revealed what was needed to be known. Nothing else existed.

The page was a yellow and dry canvas. Soon lines appeared, intersected, and took shape. Some lines made pictures, others formed letters. Damon read slowly, committing every stroke to memory.

It was a warning, but not about a Mithughee strike team as Damon expected. A God of the Near and his followers were plotting to take Rebecca from them and make sure she did not survive the night. The book even gave him a name. Yeh-Rholyu.

Damon suppressed a laugh. Yeh-Rholyu was an aged and underfed Near God. Even his picture in *The Tome* showed him hunched and dogged.

Glass crashed downstairs. Gracie and Chris screamed things that Damon didn't hear well enough to understand.

Damon skimmed the remaining pages and ran out of the room.

He jumped over the railing of the staircase, landing with a soft pat on the hardwood, then darted into the living room.

Once there, he saw Gracie dive over the couch with a kitchen knife in her hand. She cursed and something scurried into the dining room.

"What is going on?" Damon yelled.

"Something bit the back of Chris's leg," Gracie said. "It was on Rebecca a second ago, but I lost it."

"What did it look like?" Damon asked.

Gracie stood over Rebecca, knife at the ready. "Like some sort of spider or cat."

"Those are two very different things."

"I didn't get a good look at it."

"Clearly," Damon said.

"Do you sense anything?"

Damon reached out and heard the rhythm of thought, but it was garbled, as though listening to someone talk while under water. He understood the tone of the thinker's intentions. They were commands. "Someone's controlling it."

A plate flew across the room and shattered against Gracie's head. She slumped over the coffee table and grew still.

Damon's eyes traced the path of the plate to the thing on the dining room table. Eight to ten inches tall. Dark fur. Five legs. Bulbous eyes and bat ears. It parted its lips and let out a low growl through small, sharp teeth.

He lunged for it, but it leapt over him and hurled itself out of the already broken window. Damon followed, shattering more of the glass out onto the back patio.

He landed on the stone and watched as the thing scurried along the wall of the house next door. He took a breath and did the same.

It ran around garbage cans and between houses.

It slid under cars and into people's backyards.

Damon chased it as best he could without being seen, but when it shot along a wire to a rooftop bar across Fourteenth Street, he knew he'd been beaten.

It was in his moment of quiet defeat when Damon realized that he'd been lured away from the house. If he planning an attack, this was how he would have done it.

He cursed and sprinted home.

Less than a minute later, Damon ran up the front stairs to find the door wide open. He crept inside and stalked into the living room. Gracie was on the couch with ice on her head. Chris stood over her with a dishrag around his ankle.

"Where is she?" Damon asked.

"When I got in here, she was gone," Chris said.

"She walked out. I saw her leave, but couldn't stop her. I couldn't even stand. Find her, Damon. They'll kill her if you don't find her."

Without a word, Damon leapt out of the house and onto the sidewalk. If Rebecca had her senses about her still, she'd head toward the taxi pickup point by the train station downtown.

The night had picked up since they left the bar. Thursday nights always did in Hoboken. Yet, in spite of the hordes of chubby girls with too-early tans and muscular guys with skinny legs, finding one person in a crowd was not as hard as Damon first thought it would be.

From thirty feet away, he saw Rebecca stumble and fall over the railing of the only good Thai place in the city.

By the time he ran up to her, she'd picked herself up, ignored the new scrapes on her knees and hands, and pushed on downtown. He caught her by the arm as she fell again.

That was when he heard the siren.

"Sir, would you please step back from the lady," the voice said over the car's speaker. Two doors opened and Damon's extra sense bristled with the high-tempo beat of their harmonized assumptions.

"Sir, please step back from the lady," the officer repeated.

"If I let her go, she'll fall," Damon said.

"Let her down gently, then," a younger, wider officer said. He watched Damon while the older officer helped Rebecca sit on the stone steps of a pizza place on the corner. "Do you know this woman?"

"No."

As if on command, Rebecca looked up and asked, "Damon, what's happening to me?"

"Are you Damon?" the older officer asked.

Damon nodded.

"She seems to know you, Damon," the younger officer smirked. "Again. Do you know this woman?"

"Barely," Damon said.

"First *no*, now *barely*," the older officer said, shaking his head. "Are you a friend, a brother, a husband? How much has she had to drink tonight?"

"I don't know," Damon said. "I saw her fall back there and helped her up."

"Her eyes are dilated," the older officer said. "What drugs has she taken this evening?"

"Again, I don't know," Damon said. "I just saw her fall."

A loud squawk came over the

older officer's radio. "Car seven, report."

The younger officer nodded to his elder and reached for the radio clipped on his uniform. "We've got an 11-41 on the corner of First and Hudson."

"What's that mean?" Damon asked.

"She needs to go to the ER," the older officer said. "Would you happen to know anything about her head wound?"

"No."

The man looked from his younger partner to Damon and said, "What about all of that blood on your sleeve?"

"I didn't notice it," Damon said, still looking forward. He felt their net of questions draw tighter around him.

"It's dry blood, too," the younger officer said. "How long ago did she hit her head?"

"I don't know that either."

"You're a wealth of information, Damon," the older officer said. "May we see your driver's license?"

"I don't carry ID," Damon said. "Am I under arrest or am I free to leave?"

The younger one chuckled, then said, "Well, you lied to us and you're wrist-deep in blood. What do you think?"

It was in that moment when Damon first considered killing both police officers. He looked around at the twenty bystanders and knew that if he did that he'd have to kill all of them, too.

"Again, officers," Damon asked. "Am I under arrest?"

"We're going to need to ask you a few more questions, Damon," the younger officer said. "Fortunately the station is right over there, so it's no inconvenience."

"If you're detaining me further, I want my lawyer present."

"Call whoever you want," the older officer said. "We've got all night."

Chapter Four

Some jobs are callings. That is the way Alvaro Ahmad felt every night he woke up. He'd rise from a motel bed or the backseat of his car, stop off at a diner for black coffee, toast, and a poached egg, and read through the posts for just the right assignment.

Demon worshipers, were-creatures, tomb excavations, a good Mithughee did them all. No job was too small because, as he learned early in his career, any small thing can lead to mass extinctions if left unchecked. Just ask your neighborhood vampire, if you could find one.

A young waitress with a butterfly tattoo under her ear refilled his coffee.

"You done with your eggs?"

He passed the plate to her with his left hand. She took it from him and he winced a little from the movement, though not enough for her to seem like she noticed.

Alvaro slid his right hand underneath his coat and patted the bruises on his ribs. Whatever he had killed last night hadn't matured enough to grow claws yet. That was the difference a proactive approach made in this kind of work—bruised ribs were a hell of a lot better than a torn ribcage. Not even close.

It took time to learn which assignments could be handled with an hour's knife work and which required a team of hunters. He was alone today. Injured and alone. So he sipped his coffee and scrolled through the list for something light.

That was when he read the post from his assigner.

STEPHANIE POWELL: Case 856: Hudson County, NJ. Code 8 - Track and Follow. Possible Artifact Recovery of Item #54326. 2MC.

Alvaro knew those numbers. Item #54326 was *The Tome of Testaments*, a book he had lost track of thirteen years ago. The goddamn thing was dangerous, more than the Central Humanist Collective gave it credit for being. The CHC was good at organizing the mortal power players, the Mithughee included. Without a united front, mankind would have died a horrid death a hundred times over in as many years. But with that organization came caution and hesitation.

He lifted his left arm and the tight soreness crept around his side. *Track and Follow*, the post read. He decided that he could stake it out for the night, especially if it was a 2MC. At least a Mithughee presence would give the job

an appropriate sense of seriousness.
He thumbed his response to the post.

ALVARO AHMAD: Interested in 856. It's 2MC so who's the second Mithughee?

STEPHANIE POWELL: Randall Sefack.

Something close to a smile crept across Alvaro's face. He hadn't seen Randall since the kid took his rites three years ago. New Jersey wasn't that far away, three hours maybe. It'd be great to catch up with his old protégé and maybe bring in *The Tome of Testaments* while they were at it.

Many Mithughee stuck to rural mountains or dense forests. That was the old mentality.

Long ago, man ran naked through the trees and felt a connection to nature. Yes, nature existed in the woods, but gods and men buried their secrets and built over them. Villages grew into forts. Forts gave way to tombs. Castles became government buildings or libraries or hospitals. Multi-million dollar vaults and comparably costly government bribes were so commonplace in our large cities that their absence would be noticed far more quickly than their presence.

Randall knew all of this and Alvaro had made sure he learned it well. The cities were where all hell could break loose at any moment. A good hunter belonged there.

ALVARO AHMAD: I'm in. Send me his pendant's tracking key.

STEPHANIE POWELL: Key #986. Post 856 Now Filled.

Alvaro dropped a twenty on the table and headed to his car.

Chapter Five

Damon sat in a cold room for three hours before Chris leaned in and waved him out. "Come on. Let's go."

"That's it?" Damon asked.

Chris shrugged. "The magic of a law degree."

"What were they holding me for?"

"Possible assault and obstructing an investigation," Chris said. "Don't lie to cops."

Damon grunted. He pushed past Chris into the hallway and made for the front door. The two officers who brought him in stopped talking and watched him as he left. Damon didn't turn back until he reached the sidewalk outside of the station. "Am I being charged?"

"They tried to make it sound like that," Chris said, limping after him. "We need to get you an ID. The cops may need to get a hold of you if her injuries turn out to be suspect."

"Which they're going to be."

"They'll no doubt raise an eyebrow," Chris said. He took a step and winced.

"How're you doing?"

"Been better. Gracie had already patched me up, but it still took a while to hobble over here and get you straight. We lost valuable time."

Chris handed Damon a cellphone. "They sent her to Hoboken University Medical Center. She should still be there."

"Got it," Damon said. "Go home, Chris."

Chris nodded and lurched up Hudson Street toward the house.

The hospital was only a few blocks north and west.

Damon made it to Washington Avenue and had only just worked out his approach when a voice came from behind him.

"Hey, wait up."

Damon looked back at a wiry man with a badge on his belt. The beat of his surface thoughts were measured and deliberate. "My lawyer just left, officer," Damon said. "If you want to talk, it'll be through him."

The man smiled and breathed a quiet laugh. "I'd heard you had some training in dealing with police."

"Then I'm free to go?"

"Not yet." The cop held out his phone and nodded his head towards it. "You're going to want to see this."

Damon leaned in and watched the screen go black. Little dots circled as the video loaded. It was a high angle of a man and a woman in an alley. The man had a grip on the woman and spun her around. She fought back, but he hit her in the stomach. The woman fell and hit her head on the asphalt.

"That's your Rebecca," the cop said. "And that's how she got her head wound." Damon's heart raced as he noticed that there was another thirty seconds left in the video. The cop grinned. "Wait for it."

Damon looked back at the screen as a second man ran into view, grabbed the first one, and slammed him into the dumpster.

Then the second man *changed*. He grew larger and became something different, something greater.

There was a blur of movement. The first man fell and the video ended.

"How did you get this?" Damon asked.

The cop thumbed the touch screen and deleted the video. "Get what?"

"Am I supposed to think that's the only copy?" Damon asked.

"I have as much to lose here as

you do."

"How did you know where to look?"

"Spirits are excellent informants," the cop smiled.

"The couple," Damon said with an exhale. He hardened himself. "What do you want?"

"This isn't about blackmail."

"You're not disturbed by what you saw?"

"Not at all," the cop said. "Quite the opposite, actually. We're excited. Whatever it is that you are, you're exactly what we've been looking for."

"We?" Damon asked.

"That's right," the cop said. "I haven't introduced myself." He rolled up his sleeve to the elbow and pointed to an intricate scar-too on his forearm. "I'm Lieutenant Kevin Holmes of the Hoboken Police Department and Chief Field Officer of the Rholyites."

Damon laughed out loud. "Yeh-Rholyu is an old and tired thing, clinging to life on what little scraps the other Near Gods give him."

The lieutenant recoiled. The tempo of his measure quickened and his beat became a stiff percussion. "Far God myths have warped your view of reality. They're all gone now. They've returned to the source millennia ago. Trithuko. Mulsfenu. Dloigotha. Dæmñrœ."

"You're not pronouncing that right," Damon seethed.

"Does it matter?" Kevin asked, waving at the swarms of people. "You're not doing anything out in the open. The time of the Near Gods is at hand."

With those words, Damon saw that the lieutenant's dark hand had deep creases around the wrist that resembled eyes and a mouth that looked like the cat-spider from earlier. "We've met already."

"Nearly," Kevin smirked. "You're faster than you look."

"Controlling your hand from afar is a neat trick."

The lieutenant shrugged, "Comes with experience."

"What did you do to her?"

"A little sting," he said. "It secretes a faint scent I can trace if I need to."

Damon's voice grew cold. "Leave her alone."

"I can't promise that," Kevin said. "She means something to you and we're curious why."

"It's none of your concern," Damon said.

"I doubt that." The lieutenant rolled his sleeve down and fastened his cuff. "Followers of the Far Gods come into our territory and take an interest in one particular person? Something is up."

"We've been here for longer than you think," Damon said.

"All the more reason to be suspicious," Kevin said. "Why would you start getting careless now? What is it about her that is so important?"

"Stay away from her."

"Again, no promises."

"You want promises? I'll make you a promise." A deep rage coursed through Damon's veins and he came to the edge of losing control. He pulled himself back and breathed one long slow breath. "Stay out of my way or you and your whole kind will die at my feet tonight."

Damon gave the grinning lieutenant one more hard look. Without another word, he turned toward the hospital.

Chapter Six

Warm spring nights in Hoboken smelled like a sour mix of beer, bronzer, and bile. To their credit, the ER staff at the Hoboken hospital kept most of that stench outside. It's impossible to know how they did it, considering that the people who contributed most to the city's unique bouquet ended up in their waiting room.

Damon pushed past the hellscape of twenty-somethings on his way to the front desk. "Rebecca Wilson."

"Excuse me," the woman responded. Her thoughts were a single-tone melody, soft and slow. She blinked a few times, then shook herself more alert. "What was the name?"

"Rebecca Wilson," Damon repeated.

"Are you family?"

"I'm her half-brother," Damon lied. "She was brought in earlier."

The woman typed, then stared at the screen for another few seconds. "She was discharged."

"How long ago?"

She looked at the screen again. "About a half an hour ago."

"Who picked her up?" Damon asked.

The woman gave him a hard stare. Fatigue washed from her features and her eyes sharpened. She took her hands off of the keyboard and looked Damon over in a way that told him she was memorizing his description. "You could call her to find that out," she said after her eyes reached his again. "What did you say your name was?"

"I didn't," Damon said. "Thank

you for your time."

He sped out of the hospital. The woman called out after him, but Damon was faster than your average overworked healthcare professional. She would make a note of the conversation. No matter. No amount of questioning could undo tonight's necessary work.

Rebecca must live to see the morning.

Her apartment was in Jersey City Heights, a twenty-minute walk west of the hospital. Damon covered it in three.

He slipped out of someone's overgrown backyard and onto the sidewalk on Palisade Avenue. Two people saw him and stopped talking for a breath. One asked for change for a cup of coffee. Damon gave the man a dollar and crossed the last two blocks toward Rebecca's apartment building.

Travel on foot allowed him to clear his head and make a plan. One, get into the apartment. Two, take her back to Chris and Gracie's. Three, guard Rebecca until morning.

Had he more time, the plan would have been more thorough, but time was short and she was in more than a minimum of danger. Damon stood at the corner across from Rebecca's building for a minute and set his point of entry.

Old as it was, Rebecca's apartment was the only building in the Heights with decent security. He'd been here dozens of times already.

Beginning early in the fall semester, Rebecca held study sessions on Sunday evenings. After Gracie introduced him to Rebecca as someone who might be interested in the program the following year, Damon made the occasional meeting so as not to seem too present. Each time he showed up, he took stock of their systems.

On either side and across

the street, two-family homes sat comfortably penetrable. Not this building. The doors had keycard locks and there were cameras everywhere. One over the front door. Another set over the garage and another on the far side of the building. More cameras lined the hallways, stairwells, and elevator.

Rebecca's apartment was on the second floor and her windows were right over the garage. Damon considered it. Evading one camera is a more attractive idea than evading four.

A man leaned out of a window of the house behind him, talking to no one, not even himself. One or two words would make sense, then he'd flow into a string of mumbling and curses. Damon weighed his options and wondered how this man's police report would sound read back in a courtroom.

From a standing start, he scaled the brick, tapping the ledges and holds long enough to fool anyone watching the footage later that he was just an excellent climber and not something more. He had already let his truer form get recorded once out of carelessness. He couldn't afford more mistakes. Not when *she* was relying on him.

    The window locks were, as usual, a joke. He pulled hard enough to strip the screws out of the frame and slid into the apartment.

    Once inside, he climbed down off of the couch and into the living room. He stalked past the dining room and into the hallway outside of the master bedroom.

    Damon stood comfortably in the dark and felt the night's worries drain from him. Things would be as they should be. He checked his phone. 1:28 am. He had hours to go before light. So much had happened already, but it was all worth it to know that Rebecca was safe.

It was when he stepped into the bedroom that he knew something was wrong. There was no melody. There was no beat. Cleanly folded sheets and well-placed pillows drew him to one painful and obvious conclusion—Rebecca was not here.

Her absence filled the space like an odor. He was lost, a feeling he knew well before Chris and Gracie saved him.

Damon shook his thoughts clear and set himself to figuring out his next move. What was he missing? He retraced the last four hours.

Did the woman at the hospital lie to him? No, he would have sensed that right away. Liars were the easiest to read.

The doors and windows in the apartment were intact and there was no evidence of a fight, so no one broke in before him.

Was she taken somewhere else? Rebecca never mentioned family.

Another friend from school, perhaps? The woman at the desk never told him who came to pick her up from the hospital.

She said to call her.

It was the simplest answer, one that made little sense until now, when all other options were exhausted.

Just call her.

Damon pulled his phone out of his pocket and dialed the number.

It picked up after two rings, a good sign. Damon expected that it would be turned off or have gone to voicemail. He perked up his voice. "Hey, Rebecca. It's Damon. I lost you earlier tonight and wanted to check on you?" He heard only breath. "Where are you?"

There was another pause as someone cleared their throat. "We're at the old stone house on Palisade," a low and familiar voice said. "Come alone."

Damon's heart sank to his stomach. He drew a short breath.

"Lieutenant Holmes, I don't think you realize what you are doing."

"We know exactly what we are doing."

"I mean to yourself," Damon grumbled. A rage filled him. "I will rend you."

"Yeh-Rholyu guides my actions," Kevin said.

"Then I will crush his feeble skull in my hands."

"You have twenty minutes," Kevin said. "One minute longer…"

"Start the clock, Lieutenant. Watch it closely. You'll be dead in fifteen." Damon hung up the phone and slid back outside through the living room window.

Chapter Seven

Alvaro took one hand off the wheel and reached into his shirt. He grabbed his pendant and placed a thumb on the opal center. This was the seventh time he attuned to Randall's pendant tracking key and it gave him the same result each time. Randall hadn't moved.

Three hours without contact was a bad sign, especially for assignments marked *Track and Follow*.

He slammed a palm on the dashboard. He was minutes away now and perhaps hours too late.

Randall had to have known to wait for a second man before starting the assignment, right? He had learned at least that much, hadn't he?

After twenty minutes of looking for parking, Alvaro Ahmad gave up and pulled onto Court Street. He turned off his engine, pulled a hood up over his head, and eased out of his car.

He tapped his pendant's opal twice for a location signal. The pulse of Randall's pendant answered up ahead—in the dumpster.

Alvaro looked up and down the street and at each of the windows.

There was a camera above a far window, the sole silent guardian of the street.

Alvaro whispered into his pendant and waited for the events of the world to make the camera inoperable for him.

Satisfied, he walked to the dumpster. He didn't give himself time to build concern or worry over what he was about to find. He just opened the damn thing.

There was a thin layer of trash. Beneath that, Randall's torn and broken body lay twisted and cold.

Alvaro breathed one hard sigh before checking his wounds. Claw marks across the chest and torso. Crushed bones in his hands. He turned the body over and found his Hklfeha dagger underneath him. Whoever did this had to have known not to rob the body after killing him. There weren't many who fit that description and even fewer who could cause this type of damage. If *The Tome of Testaments* was involved, then that left only one. Damon Nero.

A ripple of excitement overtook Alvaro as the possibility of retaking the book became a greater and greater probability. If Damon Nero was here, then *The Tome of Testaments* couldn't be far at all. It could even be in this city, hidden away in one of its many corners.

Alvaro stood over Randall for a moment longer out of respect. He raised Randall's Hklfeha dagger and drove the hilt of it down on the pendant around Randall's neck. The opal cracked and a dark mist rose out of its setting. It surrounded the dead Mithughee in thin wisps. Alvaro dropped the dagger in the dumpster and closed the lid as the cloud swallowed his former protégé. This life may be over for Randall, but he'll need his dagger in the next.

Alvaro climbed back in his car and smiled. A small hope grew in him that Randall would be his mentor when it was his turn to pass through.

A different hope grew. Damon Nero was close by and so was *The Tome of Testaments*. With the right support and a little luck, this thirteen-year case could be nearing its end.

Alvaro Ahmad backed out of Court Street and drove off to find parking in Hoboken.

CHAPTER EIGHT

Every*thing* that's any*thing* knew the stone house on Palisade Avenue. It's the only three-hundred-year-old house in the Heights, a real point of interest in the area. Curious, considering that three hundred years wasn't that much time.

Ancient cultures laugh at the people of this continent. Three hundred years ago, European castles and tombs were centuries-old relics. Asian and African temples were dust and ruin millennia before that. But Americans rarely let things grow old.

Damon let himself think on this for a few seconds of blissful distraction while a more serious question burned in the back of his mind. Why was Yeh-Rholyu interfering? He had to have known who Damon was, even if the lieutenant said his name without knowing it.

These thoughts puzzled Damon in the forty-five seconds he took to sprint the distance from Rebecca's building to the stone house.

Once he was on the block, he slowed. Kevin and whoever else Yeh-Rholyu was working with were ready for him.

Damon stood on the rooftop next to the house. What surprises did they have planned? The house was small, too small to hide enough troops to concern him. Maybe it was just Kevin and Yeh-Rholyu, or was that too easy? It had been too long since he felt a Near God's lifeblood on his talons.

A faint buzz came from the phone in his pocket. Damon reached in and read the text.

CHRIS: Update?

Damon thought about ignoring it, but decided better. Chris would keep texting if he didn't get an answer. He tapped the screen.

DAMON: Stone house on Palisade. Yeh-Rholyu. One hour.

He then turned off his phone and slid it back into his pocket.

The front door was most likely the least guarded, but it was the most public and Damon couldn't afford the attention of a shootout with a police lieutenant on a busy city street. Nor could he risk being seen kicking in the door of a point of interest.

The window it was.

He stepped off of the ledge and clung to the stone house beside the second-story window. He pulled the window open with two fingers, then crept into the house.

Damon looked around the bedroom for any planned defenses and found none. No alarms. No cameras as far as he could tell. No weapons.

There were several parts of the room that struck Damon as odd. The drawers in the dresser were ajar, the closet doors were half open, and the bed was unmade. Damon touched the still-warm pillow. Someone left in a hurry, probably the surrogate owners of the house, the people Yeh-Rholyu used to preserve it over the centuries.

The bedroom door was open enough to see into the hallway. The other two doors on the second floor were shut and there was a light on at the top of the stairs.

Damon quieted himself. He felt around for others with a sense that was more touch than sight or sound and found the pleasant tempo of a spiked heart rate. Although he couldn't pry into his host's thoughts, the lieutenant's flat pitch was unmistakable.

The man was alone.

Curiosity overtook Damon. Part of him wanted to drop down and sneak up behind his prey, but he decided to be more direct.

When he reached the first floor, he saw a light on behind the stairs toward the back of the house. He stepped into the kitchen and found Kevin sitting at the table, staring at his phone. Cheap coffee filled the air and the lieutenant sipped his cup.

"Am I interrupting?" Damon asked, watching the man's eyes.

Kevin saw him and stiffened. His face drained of color. He lowered his cup and phone to the table. "I get so few moments to myself," he said. "But, no. You're right on time."

Damon felt the joyful spike of fear that overtook the lieutenant ebb. The drop was slow, but definite, as though the anticipation of the moment concerned him more than the moment itself.

Kevin checked his watch. "I'm

still alive."

"It's only been eight minutes since we talked," Damon said. "You've got time."

Kevin smiled and sipped his coffee again.

"Where is she?"

"Just like that?" Kevin said, putting his cup down on the table. "No threats? No beatings? No torture?"

"I always start light."

"Very kind of you."

"It's not kindness," Damon said. "It's expediency."

"I get it," Kevin said. "We're all busy."

"Your schedule is going to clear up."

"So you do start with threats," Kevin said. He loosened his watch and put it on the table. "One thing first."

Damon nodded.

"Why her? What makes her so special?"

"The usual," Damon smirked. "Born under the right stars. The perfect shade of eye color. The proper lineage. A pure heart. What does it matter to you?"

Kevin shifted in his seat. "I just wanted to know what it was we were taking from you. I want to know what I'll be feeding to Yeh-Rholyu."

Damon grabbed Kevin by his coat and lifted him from his chair. The man was far lighter than he expected and, even though Damon didn't lift him above the man's usual height, he carried most of the man's weight.

It was then that Damon saw that Kevin had no legs. They had fallen from the lieutenant and were now on the floor. But instead of lying there, they shuffled out of their pant legs and grew legs of their own. Their hip joints became mouths full of teeth and each foot became a barb like that of a scorpion.

One of these barbs struck Damon in the thigh.

"What the hell?" Damon said, kicking at the leg that stung him.

"Just a few more surprises for you," Kevin said. His hand, the one that attacked Rebecca earlier, crept down Damon's arm and bit him on the wrist.

Damon dropped the man and, as the lieutenant's body hit the floor, his body split further. He became different things, almost unrecognizable as a head, two arms, and a torso. Each piece of Kevin, six in total now, scuttled about the house in all directions.

The man's arm slithered underneath the table and behind the couch in the living room.

Damon stormed out of the kitchen after it. As he reached the threshold into the living room one of Kevin's hands, covered in thick black fur, dropped off of the wall and scratched his face. It hissed, then disappeared under the stairs before Damon could catch it.

The lieutenant's now thin

and raspy voice filled the room. "Surprised?"

"More than I should have been," Damon said, wiping the blood off of his face. "I'm more surprised that you can talk without lungs."

"It isn't pleasant," Kevin rasped.

"Well, get used to it, because I'm removing them tonight."

Something low to the floor ran in front of the stairs and into the dining room. A chair slid and Damon followed the sound.

He walked more cautiously into the room this time, expecting another attack. Instead, the thin voice met him. "It is taking you a lot longer to kill me than you said."

"I'm not killing you yet," Damon whispered.

A searing pain struck Damon's ankle. He kicked at it, but caught only a glimpse of an arm, or what was an arm, as it slithered under an end table.

There was a laugh. "Not like that,

you're not."

"If I wanted it, you'd be dead already," Damon said. "I need you alive. Where is she?"

Gentle tapping above Damon's head alerted him to the next attack. He dropped to a knee and looked up in time to see the scorpion-leg drop from the ceiling. Damon crashed to the floor. The spiny legs dug into his arms and torso, but that wasn't what concerned him. Damon watched the barb at the end of this malformed extremity.

It struck and Damon jerked his head left in time to avoid the sting. The barb stuck in the wood. It jerked twice to free itself. Damon bit deep into what would under normal circumstances be the heel of Kevin's leg. A shriek came from the mouth of the thing. From a different location, the man also screamed.

Damon squeezed the thing on him and felt a few bones crack. It went limp in his arms and Kevin screamed again.

Damon pushed the broken ugliness off of him and stood upright. "Again, where is she?"

There was no answer.

"What?" Damon asked. "Nothing to say now?"

He drew into himself and felt for a pulse in the house. An odd measure greeted him. The lieutenant's flat pitch and rapid beat came in a chorus, a horrible cacophony to match his many parts.

Damon tried working the old-fashioned way.

He pushed the couch over and a snake-arm jumped at his head. He snatched it out of the air and cracked the first long bone he felt.

A scream came from the next room.

He twisted it until the bone ripped through the skin.

More screams followed from the same location.

"I'm getting tired of asking."

Damon walked past the couch and the front of the stairs into the dining room. There, under the table, several of the lieutenant's parts were in a heap.

Damon dropped the arm and kicked it off to the side. He then threw two of the chairs out of the room and drove a fist into the center of the table. The wood splintered and broke clean down the middle. The two halves fell to their sides, creating a narrow opening in the center of the room.

In clear view, Damon watched Kevin's head and torso reattach. The unbroken arm and leg did the same. With greater effort and pain, the crushed leg and arm crept their way over to the body.

Damon knelt beside the broken man. "Now, one last time."

The lieutenant laughed.

Damon smiled. "You are sunnier than you showed in our first few conversations."

ADVERSARY

"That's not it," Kevin said. He pointed with his good arm at the trail of blood.

Damon looked at the floor. Someone else, someone mortal, would have seen the wavy lines and hard angles as the pained twisting streaks of broken limbs, but Damon noticed the pattern right away. It was a symbol. The mark of Yeh-Rholyu.

Damon laughed. "If all it took to summon your tired old god was smearing your blood on the floor, I'd have gotten around to it sooner."

Kevin laughed again, but this time it was weaker and sounded more satisfied than amused. The man's eyes became glassy and distant. In their reflection, Damon watched as a rolling cloud of black mist swallowed the street, the house, everything.

The room became dark, but not in any natural way. The darkness ambushed him. It wrapped him up like a blanket, muffling all light and sound.

Damon spoke into the darkness. His words come out as a stifled whisper. "This is how you hide in your final moments, Yeh-Rholyu?"

He reached out with his senses. There was fear, which was good, but there was also an eagerness that filled the room, as potent as the darkness itself.

"What are we so excited about?" Damon said into the black curtain around him. An answer came and, even though he hardly heard his own words, the voice was clear and loud.

"You," the voice said. "I'm excited to have you."

Something grabbed Damon around the neck and pulled him further into the void.

CHAPTER NINE

There were hands on him.
Not hands.
They grabbed him. Pulled him. Battered him. His wrist snapped.
Damon clutched his arm as the bone mended.
His sight returned to him, but not because the darkness receded. His eyes adjusted to it somehow, but with his sight came the immediate concern over where he was. All things were a deep shimmering gray, as though he were underwater at dusk. He looked to Kevin, but all he saw was the lieutenant's shadow.
What is this place? Damon thought.

A voice rose to meet him. "We are beneath the lie you know. A Near God realm, one of many."

Damon followed the voice with his eyes. There, by the front door, stood a small man. He leaned on the banister of the staircase and held a handkerchief to his mouth. He coughed once into it, then looked up at Damon with baggy, red eyes.

The small figure shifted his weight further onto the banister and cleared his throat. "You see parts of it when you change. Glimpses. Here, we are all, all of us, aware."

Damon looked around him. "There's no one here but us."

"Not now, there isn't," Yeh-Rholyu said. "Not while I hunt."

"Hunt? You can barely stand."

"Are the other Far Gods in better shape?" A smirk crawled across his gray face. "Ah, yes. Your girl is supposed to fix this for you." Yeh-Rholyu coughed a dry laugh. "Odd how we are all dependent on the actions of lesser things."

"Where is she? If you've hurt her..."

"You'd do what? Slay me?" Yeh-Rholyu asked.

"That's my line in the sand."

The god's brow furrowed. "You're what?"

"My line in the sand," Damon repeated. "If you cross a line in the sand, there is no going back. It's a common saying now."

"I don't keep up," Yeh-Rholyu said. "Needless to say, yes, I have hurt her and I will continue hurting her as long as it amuses me." The God of the Near stood upright and stretched his arms, all of his arms. A sound like rubber on plastic crackled as Yeh-Rholyu showed his true self. His beige and slick body stood motionless as jointed chitinous limbs writhed like a dozen expectant fingers.

Yeh-Rholyu raked one of his

limbs across the floor in front of him, cutting a deep groove in the wood. "She is mine now."

"Is that your line?" Damon asked.

"I was hoping you would get my meaning," Yeh-Rholyu said. "We have no sand in the house."

~

"Are you sure that he said nothing else?" Gracie asked as she walked up to *The Tome of Testaments*. The book's pages ruffled as she opened it.

Chris hung back and watched her work. "Just that it was Yeh-Rholyu and he's in the Heights. I've been trying him since, but he must have turned off his phone."

"The book is showing me what it knows about Yeh-Rholyu now," Gracie said. She studied the words in silence until she let out a horrified gasp.

"What is it?" Chris asked, rushing up behind her. "How do we stop Yeh-Rholyu?"

"I can't, not anymore," she said. "And if you're reading over my shoulder, neither can you."

Chris's eyes reached the bottom of the page. He shook his head and frowned. "Son of a bitch. Does Damon know?"

"Maybe, but we were being attacked. He might not have read all the way through," Gracie said. "How did he sound on the phone?"

"I told you it was a text, but it's Damon. He's going to kill him."

"Which is exactly what Yeh-Rholyu wants."

~

Glass shattered.

Damon was airborne until he hit something not as hard as he was. It splintered. He landed and discovered a young branch beneath him. The tree he crashed into split down the middle and sagged in the grass.

Grass?

Damon looked up at the house

he was just thrown from and the field that surrounded it. He was on Palisade Avenue, or at least he should have been. All around, grass and trees replaced the cityscape that should have greeted him.

Yeh-Rholyu peered out from the shattered window. "Don't be alarmed."

"What is this? The past?"

"Not at all." The god's writhing limbs recoiled as he dismissed the idea. "Time moves as it does anywhere else."

"Because this is the truth beneath the lie?" Damon asked with a sneer.

"Right."

"You still have your house," Damon said. Glass fell from his clothes as he stood.

"It is old and the truth has accepted it." Yeh-Rholyu climbed out of the house and examined Damon. "You killed that tree."

"The tree was in the middle of

ADVERSARY 77

the street," Damon said. "Someone chopped it down a century ago."

"Its spirit lived on here. If it had been standing in the lie you know, it would wither and fall in days."

"So killing something there doesn't kill its spirit here, but killing something here destroys it completely?"

"In absolute."

"Then we're in the right place." Damon called on his *truer* form. The strength of it rushed through his veins, flooding his senses. The grass and dirt beneath his feet sunk in under his new weight.

Yeh-Rholyu stretched his tendrils out and coiled them expectantly.

The two nightmares snarled and spat at one another.

Damon pounced.

~

Chris never teased Gracie for being a terrible driver. Coming of age on the Jersey Shore gave her a prolonged adolescence, a sense of immortality that grew in proportion to her recklessness. So when she clipped a parked car on Newark Avenue, Chris said nothing about it.

"He's still not picking up," Chris said, putting the phone down on his lap.

Gracie's eyes narrowed. She pressed her foot down harder and the engine grunted in anger. "We have to get to him."

"You know how he gets when he's... determined," Chris said.

"It doesn't matter," Gracie said. "Whoever kills Yeh-Rholyu will be cursed to live out his sentence straddled between worlds. He'll be separated from her forever."

Gracie sped into the Heights and parked in front of the first fire hydrant on Palisade Avenue. She cut the engine and raced to the old stone house.

Chris hobbled behind her.

She was already halfway through a shattered window by the time he caught up to her.

He waited for her to open the door for him.

Chris walked into the living room and counted the scrapes along the wall and ceiling. "What a mess."

Gracie's voice came in from around the corner. "Over here."

Chris climbed over the broken and bloodied furniture. "That must be the symbol of Yeh-Rholyu. Did Damon do this?"

"I'm not sure," Gracie said. "It doesn't look like his blood. It's too thin."

Chris pointed to the body in the corner. "Maybe it belongs to him?"

Gracie knelt down over the man and picked through his pockets. She opened his wallet and a gold badge dropped to the floor.

Chris sighed. "He promised not to kill any more cops."

"And you were expecting him to just stop?" Gracie asked. "These are old habits."

"The world is different now," Chris said. "He can't just go one town over, change his name, and expect that people will move on."

"Well, you can relax," Gracie said, pulling her hands back from the man's neck. "He's alive."

"Even better, a cop who can write a description of his attacker," Chris huffed. "I'm guessing that this is his blood all over the floor."

"Was that a question?" Gracie asked.

"Not really," Chris said. "But if Yeh-Rholyu was behind this and he was summoned in front of Damon, why is this house still standing? Don't get me wrong, this place is a disaster, but the damage here is only a part of Damon's warm-up routine."

Gracie shrugged. "Maybe they left?"

"Yeah," Chris said looking around

the room. "But where could they have gone?"

~

A black claw whistled through the air, slicing off a length of Yeh-Rholyu's tendril. It fell to the grass and twitched before going still.

The old god cried out, slinking away. "I'll tell you where she is."

Damon stalked closer. "It isn't about just that anymore."

Yeh-Rholyu's rich yellow eyes grew wide. He turned and crawled back toward the house in haste. Several lengths of his body reached into the ground and wrapped around posts to pull him faster. Two arms dragged his body across the grass while others grasped at the next holds. He moved quickly this way in spite of his injuries.

Damon smiled at the trail of slick blood and slowed his gait to match Yeh-Rholyu's speed. A pleasant trill of sadism rippled through him. Even though Damon didn't feel that he needed his gift to tell him that Yeh-Rholyu was afraid, he tapped into it anyway.

The fullness of the silence stopped him cold.

Instead of a panicked tenor or the solid low tones of planning or even a bargainer's baritone, there was the constant beat of the old god's pulse.

Unsatisfied, Damon stoked his adversary's furnace. "How long has it been since you felt fear? A century? Longer?" He added to this by digging a claw into one of Yeh-Rholyu's trailing appendages. The old god screamed.

Pain was a valuable addition to the music of terror. Like a cymbal crash, it was beautiful in concert with other instruments. Alone, it was cheap and over too quickly.

As the noise faded, however, it left behind a soft melody so high and so light it could have been overlooked. Damon listened to these faint tones of wonder for a full measure.

There was an itch of a thought. Damon pushed it away.

Yeh-Rholyu made it back into the house.

Damon followed.

In the constant glow of this world, the trails of blood that the good lieutenant left behind shone, looping and intersecting in an intricate circle. Yeh-Rholyu slid into the dining room and positioned himself in the center of the markings.

The itch grew into an annoyance. He again dismissed it and advanced on the bloodied god.

Damon raised his hand and, as he struck, his mind lurched forward. The attack at the house. Rebecca's kidnapping. The constant antagonism of the police lieutenant. Luring him to this house and crossing him over to this world.

Me, Damon thought. *This was all to get me to kill Yeh-Rholyu.* Damon's final thought hit before his strike landed. *Yeh-Rholyu wants to die.*

Just as the realization came to him, his claws glanced off of the old god's face, sparking as they connected.

"No!" Yeh-Rholyu howled. A force pulsed from him, sending Damon through the wall between the kitchen and the dining room.

Damon shook the drywall off of him and stood. He took three steps before his senses told him that they had crossed back from behind the veil. Man's lights and loudness greeted him and the air was heavy again with the burdens of his inventions.

He pushed his way through the hole he made back into the dining room and found Yeh-Rholyu sprawled on the floor, sobbing.

"Damon, don't," Gracie's voice screamed.

Damon looked over at her. "What are you two doing here? Get out!"

"We all have to leave," Gracie said. "It's a curse. If you kill him, you'll be—"

A tendril slammed her against a wall. The woman slumped to the floor.

Chris charged Yeh-Rholyu with a broken table leg. He swung and the wood splintered in his grip. Yeh-Rholyu reached out and battered the man unconscious.

Damon swiped at him, but this time his talons broke against the old god's skin. He struck again and felt the bones in his massive fist shatter.

Yeh-Rholyu drove a tendril into Damon's chest and another two deep into each of his shoulders. He lifted Damon up and pinned him against the ceiling. Two more tendrils lifted Chris and Gracie and coiled around their throats.

"You can no longer hurt me, Dæmñrœ," Yeh-Rholyu said. "Your knowledge of my curse makes me immune to you from this point onward." He pushed harder into Damon's wounds. "None of you are of any further use to me."

Damon bit down and gritted through the pain. His strength seeped from him as his blood pooled on the floor. He was weak—changing back to his human disguise. His hands, now small and frail, scratched at Yeh-Rhoylu's many arms. "How is this possible?"

"How is anything possible? My curse is as it has been for over two hundred and fifty years," Yeh-Rholyu said. "Right here, on this spot, beneath the house. You asked when I last felt fear. Look around you. Every day I wake up and draw breath in New Jersey brings new horrors."

"You underestimate humans," Damon said. "Mankind is wholly ignorant. They are weak, but their machines are getting stronger. Soon, they'll discover us all—Near and Far God alike—and create new, more powerful devices."

"One can dream," Yeh-Rholyu

said. The tension in his brow eased. "Do you really think so?"

"It is only a matter of time," Damon said. "Cherish your days, old one. They are few."

A smile crept across Yeh-Rholyu's face. "This is about *her*, isn't it?"

"All things are about *her*," Damon said. "Every death. Every promise."

Yeh-Rholyu sighed. "To have someone work so hard to please you."

The old and tired god lowered Damon to the floor and withdrew his tendrils. He then lowered Chris and Gracie down beside Damon and released them.

The end of one of Yeh-Rholyu's limbs coiled around a small latch in the floor. He lifted it and a second arm raised the trap door. He lifted Rebecca out of the cellar and placed her beside the three of them. "Take her."

She strained against the ropes that held her. Her eyes bulged and she screamed through her gag.

Gracie stirred awake and cut the ropes at Rebecca's hands and feet. "She's in shock. No broken bones. No bleeding. Just a few bruises."

Damon turned to Yeh-Rholyu. "You said you hurt her."

"I said what I had to say to get you mad." Yeh-Rholyu folded in on himself and looked again like the old man Damon saw earlier. "You failed. Take her and go. Tell no one of what you learned here, especially *her*. Whatever you're up to, I want to be swept up in it without *her* knowledge."

"I'll try," Damon said.

Gracie helped Chris to his feet and they walked out of the house.

Damon grabbed a blanket off of the living room couch and draped it over Rebecca's shoulders. They made it to the car before Rebecca gathered the strength to speak in slow stutters. "My god... what... Damon."

"It's okay now," Damon said.

Tears welled in her eyes. Her

hands gripped his shirt. "What was that? Where am I?"

Damon motioned for Chris to open the car door for them. He then turned back to Rebecca. "He's not going to bother us anymore."

"I want to go home," Rebecca breathed.

"I know," Damon said. "But you can't go home."

Rebecca opened her mouth to speak but her words were cut off by a wince. She looked behind her and saw Gracie holding an empty syringe. A question formed in Rebecca's eyes before the drug took her away.

Damon caught her and guided her sleeping body into the car. "We still have a party to get to."

CHAPTER TEN

Damon, Gracie, and Chris stood naked in their living room as *The Tome of Testaments* commanded. They even had to remove all jewelry and cut off all of their bandages, which reopened Chris's leg wound from earlier.

"Do you know how loud this will be?" Gracie asked.

Damon shook his head. "The book didn't say."

"Curtains are shut," Chris said. "We're as ready as we're going to be."

A soft moan came from Rebecca as she stirred to wakefulness.

"That's our cue," Damon said. "Let's get to it."

The conversion from living space

to ceremonial chamber was faster than the layout would have led you to believe at first glance. Gracie walked to the center of the room and cleared off the oak hutch's marble top, which doubled as their altar and sometimes bar. Chris and Damon pushed most of the rest of the furniture up against the walls and laid out the drop cloths. Gracie took down the last of the picture frames, revealing the full set of painted eyes where the seven frames once were.

The three of them got to work binding Rebecca to the altar. This proved more difficult than usual because she had to be standing. That rule was clear. Damon held her upright against a five-foot 4" by 4" as Gracie and Chris tied her ankles and wrists to the hutch. Then they tied her to the board.

Rebecca was still too weak to resist them, but she spoke in her moments of greater lucidity. "What are you doing? Why are you doing this to me?" These weren't pleas, Damon noted. They were requests, questions from someone who did not yet have the presence to grasp what was happening to them.

"I know, I know," he said to her. "Quiet now. It's almost time."

"For what?" Rebecca asked.

"For you to be strong." Damon watched her for a breath longer, then took a knife and carved marks in her body.

She screamed. She jerked and pulled against her bindings.

Chris and Gracie held her while Damon slid the knife in quick movements. These had to be perfect, like an address or a telephone number. One mistake would ruin all they had worked for and sacrificed.

Damon finished the last symbol and handed the knife to Chris, who took it into the kitchen to be cleaned.

"Now what?" Gracie asked.

"Now we wait," Damon said.

Chris walked in from the kitchen drying the knife with a towel.

Several tense moments passed.

A minute ticked by, marked only by Rebecca's quiet sobbing.

Then, without warning, it happened.

Like smoldering embers, a faint light appeared in the carvings on Rebecca's body.

Light filled the room, much of which only Damon could see.

A ripple of heat washed over them and the towel in Chris's hand burst into flames. He dropped it and stomped it out. "Christ! Thank god we're not wearing clothes."

"That's why we don't question the book," Damon said.

The light became oppressive, insistent. Waves of heat pushed Gracie and Chris against the walls.

Damon switched to his truer form. Only like this could he watch. Only like this could he hold his ground against the furnace of Dloigotha.

Rebecca's hair burnt away, as did her restraints and the board behind her. Her skin rippled beneath the surface. Light pulsed throughout her body before rising to her head. There, it molded and reshaped her skull into an ornate and intricate crest of bone. She screamed in a chorus of voices as her eyes grew black.

Then, the light and heat vanished.

Dloigotha stood with her head bent forward. She flexed her fingers and stared at them.

Damon made sure that Gracie and Chris were kneeling before he walked to her. "Dloigotha, Queen Goddess of the Gnilacha Realm, Keeper of Yith-Yothoath. Your return is most glorious."

Dloigotha smiled a row of sharp teeth. "Enough, Dæmñrœ. Enough."

He smirked. "I wasn't sure how much you'd remember. It's been some time."

"Four thousand years," she said. "And I hate the Yith-Yothoath title. You know that."

"I do," Damon said. He admired her for a breath. "I nearly forgot how stunning your crown is."

"Thank you." She paused for a moment and assessed him. "You've filled out nicely in my absence."

"Food is everywhere now."

"I see," she said, gesturing to Chris and Gracie. "You live and work with them. They are your pets, or friends? Having only watched from afar, I'm sometimes confused."

"It's not you. The whole world is crazy." He stood for a moment and let his heart sing to her a song only she could hear. "What do we do now?"

She stepped forward and embraced Damon with a kiss. "Now, lover, we finish what we started millennia ago.

Chapter Eleven

Alvaro sat in his car with binoculars at his eyes and a diner cheeseburger cooling in his lap. He parked across from the house he tracked Damon Nero to in time to watch the lights stop flashing through the thick curtains. Whatever was going on just before was over now and he'd missed it.

"Track and follow," Alvaro said to himself. "That's all they needed of you tonight."

There was a soft buzz on the seat next to him.

Alvaro lowered his binoculars and picked up his phone.

STEPHANIE POWELL: Status.

ALVARO AHMAD: Transitioned Randall Sefack. Tracking Item #54326.

STEPHANIE POWELL: Transition Confirmed. Visual confirmation on Item #54326?

ALVARO AHMAD: Not yet. But I've followed Damon Nero to an address.

The "..." notification that his assigner was typing a reply came up, then went away. Alvaro waited as the pause in conversation became a full minute.

ALVARO AHMAD: This was a two-person assignment.

STEPHANIE POWELL: Two were assigned.

ALVARO AHMAD: We need more. Four should do it.

There was another pause as the "..." symbol came up, then disappeared. Alvaro started typing when the phone buzzed again.

STEPHANIE POWELL: Case 856 has been expanded. Expect a Handler to contact you within the hour.

ALVARO AHMAD: No need for a Handler.

STEPHANIE POWELL: CHC disagrees. Stand by and do not engage. Case 856 Updated.

And with that, the conversation ended.
Alvaro dropped his phone on the seat and took an angry bite from his cheeseburger. He reminded himself that it wasn't Stephanie's fault.

Assigners got their orders from the Central Humanist Collective like the rest of them.

A jogger ran along the path toward his car, a lean and fit woman in her fifties. She ran past his passenger window and continued uptown. Alvaro watched her and grew a little jealous of her ignorance. A part of him wanted to get out and run alongside her, just to talk.

He was lost in this thought when his phone buzzed again. He looked over at the seat, convinced that it must have been the Handler. They rarely wasted time and this one seemed to be as punctual as the rest he'd known. He picked up the phone and read the Handler's message. It was a location, nothing more.

Alvaro looked back up at the jogger, but she was gone along with the fantasy he had built around her. Just as well. There was little time in his life for distraction.

He took one last look at the row house on Hudson Street, then started the car and drove away. He had a lot of work ahead of him and Damon Nero was an adversary worth pursuing.

The action continues in episode 2...

BEAST

THANK YOU FOR READING.
PLEASE LEAVE A REVIEW AT
WHICHEVER OUTLET YOU
FOUND MY WORK.

IN THE MEANTME,
HERE'S A BONUS STORY
FROM MY CELEBRATED
HORROR SERIES.

WATCHING FROM BEHIND GLASS EYES

POSSESSIONS

The doll watched Margaret unpack her bags. The young girl and her family brought so many possessions with them when they moved into the old house that the doll was certain that they'd never finish. Three daylights later, they appeared to be nearly done.

It was late and the sun spilled a blood orange glow over the bedroom. The child folded and stored her belongings into one of the fancy wooden boxes that man was so fond of using.

… *dresser*, the doll thought. *That's the word.*

Words were a creation of man,

a foolish illusion of ownership.
There was a word for everything and everything had a name.

The thing watching from behind the doll's glass eyes had no name. It was born into the darkness among others and lived as one and many, legion and union. They were drawn to the creatures of the sun out of boredom, a casual and unfeeling sadism.

It was with this dangerous apathy that the thing watched Margaret, deciding how it would slay her and her family.

Suddenly, Margaret looked at the doll. Their gaze locked in silence for a few long moments and, just when the girl was about to look away, the doll tilted its head.

Very little movement was needed. Why waste energy when a tiny gesture would open the floodgates of a child's pure, rich terror?

Margaret giggled.

She was young, the doll thought scornfully. *Perhaps too young to know to be afraid.*

The thing behind the doll's glass eyes was young, too, although it didn't know how young. Numbers were another creation of man, a way to count the things they thought they possessed.

Man knew nothing of possession.

Margaret picked the doll up in her arms and held it there, pressing it to her body. She then lay the doll on the dresser next to some clothes and a glass of water.

The doll sat upright.

"No, no, Jessica," Margaret scolded as she straightened the doll out again. "Be a good girl."

Stunned into uncertainty, the doll remained still. It felt the care and concentration in the girl's hands as she dipped a piece of dry cloth in the glass of water and then dragged the now wet cloth over the doll's body.

First was the front, then the back.

Finally, the girl washed its face and eyes.

The child, now sagging with exhaustion, took the doll to her bed. She held it above her and looked deep into its shining glass eyes.

"Good night, Jessica," the girl said, hugging it tightly.

Jessica, the doll repeated silently. The word had soft and hard noises that made it almost sound like a curse if said the right way. *Jessssss-i-KA!*

It accepted the name. If it decided to let the girl live, which it did just this very moment, then it had better get used to this creature calling it a name.

The child tucked the doll beneath her arm. Her breathing slowed and she began to slip away.

Jessica, for that was the doll's name now, closed its false eyelids and pretended to sleep next to its new possession.

Jeremiah Kleckner is an author and educator in New Jersey.

Sign up for his email newsletter to get invites to public events, information about upcoming new releases, and review copies of his books.

Jeremiah's Newsletter, Blog, Facebook, Twitter, and Goodreads links are all on his website. JeremiahKleckner.com

Need quick contact? Reach Jeremiah at any time on Twitter @J_Kleckner.

Made in the USA
Middletown, DE
12 September 2017